CLAUDE

at the Palace

A NICE CUP OF TEA AND A SIT DOWN

ALEX T. SMITH

HODDER

Hello!

Ooh, look who it is!
It is Claude.
Claude is a dog.
Claude is a small, plump dog.
Claude is a small, plump dog who
is *quite* the snappy dresser.

Claude

A jaunty jumper

Well polished pumps

Claude lives in a house on
Waggy Avenue with Mr and Mrs
Shinyshoes, and his best friend in
the whole world, Sir Bobblysock.

Sir Bobblysock is both a sock and
rather bobbly.

Every morning, Mr and Mrs
Shinyshoes cry, 'Toodlepip!' and
skip out to work, and that's when
the fun begins. Claude pops on
his beret and off go he and Sir
Bobblysock on a jolly adventure.

Where
will
they
go
today?

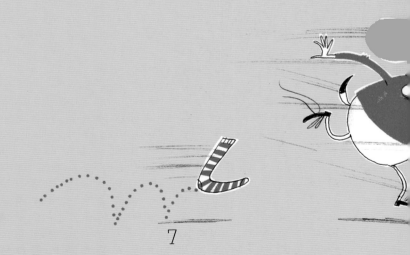

It was a Friday morning and a wet one too. It had been raining for days.

Sir Bobblysock was sitting at the window wrapped up in all his shawls, clasping a mug tightly with both hands. There was nothing in it – he just liked the overall effect.

'Ooh, Claude!' he cried. 'It's ever so damp out there! Let's just stay in today in the dry.'

But Claude had other ideas. There he was – welly boots and cagoule on, with his special little umbrella poking out of his beret.

'Don't be silly, Sir Bobblysock,'
said Claude, adjusting his toggles.
'We've been stuck in ALL week
because of the rain. We can't
waste another day's adventuring
just because it's a bit wet!'

!

Sir Bobblysock gasped. 'But my lovely bouncing curls!' he said. His flabber had never been so gasted! 'They'll go all floppy!'

'No, they won't,' said Claude. 'And besides, our treat tin is empty. There won't be any elevenses if we don't go out and find something.'

Well, THAT changed everything. Off went Sir Bobblysock's shawls, on went his plastic rain bonnet, and he was out of the door. Claude skedaddled after him.

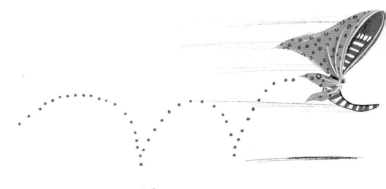

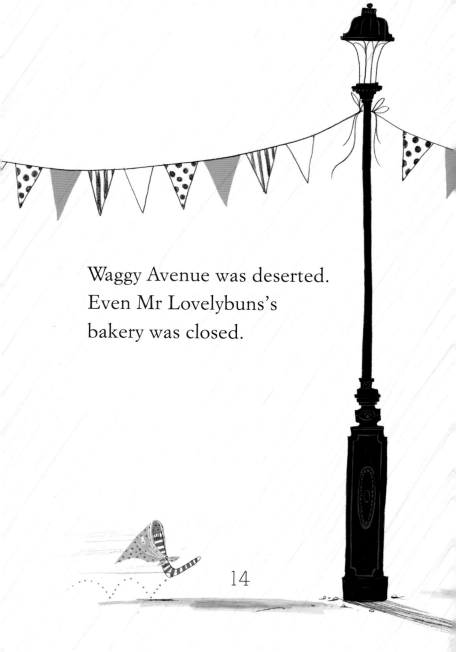

Waggy Avenue was deserted.
Even Mr Lovelybuns's
bakery was closed.

14

'Where is everyone?' asked Sir Bobblysock, his belly rumbling.

Claude didn't know, but while he thought about it he did some splish-splashing about in puddles.

When Claude looked up to tell Sir Bobblysock that he was still flummoxed, he was very surprised indeed. In front of them was a terribly fancy building with a flag fluttering above it. Mr Lovelybuns's special delivery van was parked outside.

Behind him, Claude's bottom
started to have a wiggle. Could this
be an ADVENTURE?

Then came a loud cry from within the building.

Oh dear!
Oh dear!
Oh dear!

shouted someone (in their loudest Outdoor Voice).

And before Sir Bobblysock could say, 'Oooh, Claude, I don't think you should be doing that because this building is actually the palace!' Claude had hoofed it across the drive, up the steps and through the golden front door with the big sparkly knocker.

Sir Bobblysock followed him.

Inside, smartly dressed people were dashing about in a right palaver.

Fancy chairs, blousy flowers and swags of tablecloths sailed past them. Mr Lovelybuns wobbled by with his hostess trolley, pushing the biggest cake Claude had ever seen.

'What on earth is going on?' asked Claude.

Well, it just so happened that he'd found himself right next to the person who could tell him. It was the same person who had said, 'OH DEAR!' times three earlier.

She was wearing a sparkly little crown and was holding a clipboard. Sir Bobblysock and Claude knew that the clipboard meant she was Very Much in Charge.

Claude smoothed down his cagoule and got ready to listen *very* carefully.

'Oh! I AM having a day of it,' she said. 'I'm Princess Tiara Sparkles, and today is Great Granny's birthday garden party. Very Important People are coming from all over the world to celebrate, but it's far too soggy outside, so we are moving it into the Great Hall. There's so much to do! But I'm jolly glad you are here to help...'

Claude and Sir Bobblysock blinked
like this:

BLINK!

BLINK!

BLINK!
BLINK!

24

'The royal nanny, dear Nanny Stern-Bloomers, has suddenly got one of her heads, so she's having a long lie down with a bag of frozen peas,' Princess Sparkles went on. 'Of course now there is no one to look after the Royal Children. It's very important that they are kept out of mischief and stay clean and tidy in their party outfits.'

25

Princess Sparkles stopped talking and looked at Claude and Sir Bobblysock VERY closely. 'You ARE the replacement nannies, aren't you?' she said.

Now, what Claude *should* have said here was, 'I'm sorry, but no, I am not a nanny. I am a Claude and this is a Sir Bobblysock.'

But did he?

Of course he didn't.

Claude's tail and eyebrows were waggling like billy-o. Off went his cagoule and welly boots, and from the depths of his beret came a freshly starched pinny for himself and a little lacy cap for Sir Bobblysock.

WAG!
WAG!

'Nanny Claude and Nurse
Bobblysock reporting for duty!'
cried Claude, saluting.

Princess Sparkles beamed. 'Hurrah!
Remember to keep the children
spotless. Great Granny won't stand
for ANY MESS!'

The words 'ANY MESS' were said
in capital letters and were definitely
double underlined.

Suddenly there was a very loud, very strange noise.

CREEEE

'Gosh!' exclaimed Princess Sparkles. 'That sounded like the roof of the Great Hall struggling to cope with all the rain falling on it.

EAAK!

It sounds as if it could collapse at any moment! Of course **that** wouldn't happen today though, would it?'

They all laughed heartily at **such** a silly idea, then Princess Sparkles clattered off in her court shoes to be busy elsewhere.

31

The two new nannies
marched off in the direction
of the Royal Playroom.

'Oooh, Claude...' hissed Sir
Bobblysock. 'Do you think this
is a good idea? We've never been
nannies before...'

'Don't worry, Sir Bobblysock,' said
Claude, smoothing down his pinny.
'We'll look after the children, then
we can go to the party and have
some of Mr Lovelybuns's lovely
cakes for our elevenses. It'll be
easy-peasy! Princes and princesses
are **always** on their best behaviour.'

Then he opened the door to the
Royal Playroom.

ROLL UP!
ROLL UP!
FOR the GREAT
ROYAL-BABY
CATAPULT!

Sir Bobblysock suddenly knew why
Nanny Stern-Bloomers was having a
long lie down...

Nanny Claude quickly tidied the catapult away under his beret. 'Why were you firing this baby and some jam tarts at the chandeliers?' he asked the Royal Children.

Sir Bobblysock tutted – what a way to treat pastries!

The Royal Children sighed. 'We're frightfully bored!' said Prince Bonaventure. 'We've been waiting FOREVER for the party to start.'

'We haven't been able to help at ALL with it,' Princess Debonaire explained. 'We said there should be balloons and a bouncy castle and face painting...'

'But everyone,' said Prince Beaudesert, 'ESPECIALLY Nanny Stern-Bloomers, said that Granny wouldn't like THAT sort of a party at all.'

'We weren't even allowed
to make Great Granny a
birthday card!' continued
Princess Debonaire. 'Nanny
Stern-Bloomers said we'd get
messy. She's Very Strict.'

All the children looked at
Nanny Claude with big blinking
eyes, except Prince Babyface,
who nibbled Claude's ear.

'Well, I'm MUCH jollier than
Nanny Stern-Bloomers,' said
Nanny Claude. 'And you can't
have a birthday without a
birthday card!'

He shook all his nice art supplies out of his beret and set them on the table.

'Oooh, Claude,' said Sir Bobblysock, 'I'm not sure that's a good idea. Remember the children must stay Neat and Tidy!'

'Don't worry, Sir Bobblysock!' said Claude, ferreting around in his beret. 'That's why I'm looking for my messy mat...'

There was Some Noise from behind them.

'I don't think you'll need that actually, Claude...' said Sir Bobblysock.

'Why?' asked Claude.

Then he said 'Oh,' and went all warm around the ears.

'What will we do?!' squeaked
Sir Bobblysock. 'They can't
meet kings and queens looking
like that! They are very
particular about neatness!'

'Er! Don't worry!' Claude
scrabbled about in his hat again.
'We'll use the hose. I know it's
in here somewhere.' And he
started to shake out his beret.

Out fell all his things – the jam tarts, the catapult, his spatula, his toolbox and his surfboard: The Essentials.

But as quickly as they fell
on the floor, the
Royal Children
nabbed them.

WHOOOOSH!

48

went the
surfboard.

TWANG!

went the catapult.

'WHEEEEEEEEEEE!'

giggled the baby.

SPLODGE!

went the jam tarts.

You wouldn't
believe the mess!

49

'AHA!' cried Claude, as he pulled out the hose and squirted it – SPLASH! It went EVERYWHERE.

50

Whilst the Royal Children hooted with laughter, there came a knock at the door. It was the Royal Butler to say that they must go to the Great Hall. The party had begun!

Claude quickly peeled Prince Babyface from the wall, chucked everything into his beret and led the children out of the room.

The celebrations were in full swing. All the guests were having a marvellous time, even if the party wasn't quite the sort of party Claude and the Royal Children would have organised.

Everyone looked very smart in their fanciest clothes as they clinked expensive glasses together and smiled with their teeth.

Claude and Sir Bobblysock squelched into the room with the Royal Children. They held up the paint-and-jam-splodged birthday card shyly.

Everyone gasped like this: GASP!

On her throne, Great Granny peered through her specs and cried, 'GOODNESS! I've never seen such a mess!'

Princess Tiara Sparkles put her hands on her hips. 'You were meant to keep the children Neat and Tidy...' she said.

She did not sound happy.

Then she narrowed her eyes at Claude and Sir Bobblysock.

'I have a feeling...' she said slowly, '... that you are not really royal nannies at all...'

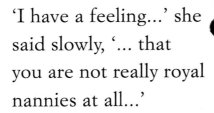

Claude combed his ears nervously. He would have to explain, but before he could say anything, two awful things happened.

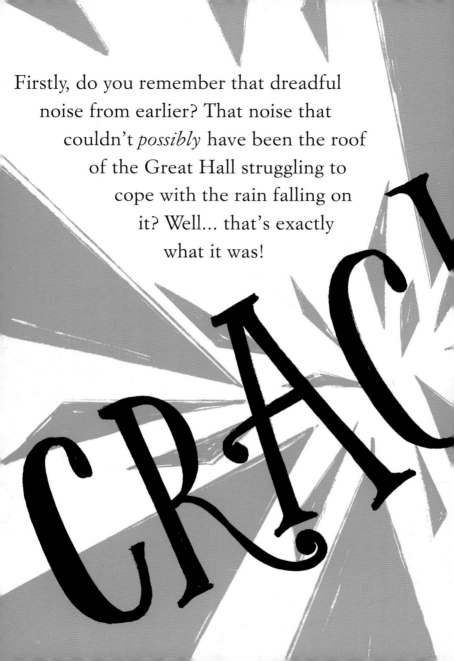

Firstly, do you remember that dreadful noise from earlier? That noise that couldn't *possibly* have been the roof of the Great Hall struggling to cope with the rain falling on it? Well… that's exactly what it was!

CRAC

A huge hole appeared
in the roof. Rain poured
into the room and everyone
ran this way and that. Sir
Bobblysock dived for
safety, landing on Great
Granny's lap.

Then the second awful thing happened.

Piles of tiles and beams tumbled down on to one end of a table, which flipped up into the air like a seesaw. It caught the edge of the golden throne and PING! fired Great Granny and Sir Bobblysock up into the air... where they landed neatly in a chandelier!

'I say!' Great Granny cried.
'Do you think someone might
rescue One?'

'Also this One too?' said Sir
Bobblysock.

Princess Tiara Sparkles was all of a quiver. 'What shall we do?' she wailed to the room in general. But nobody knew.

Claude tapped his head three times to get his brain working. Then he scratched his beret. Wait... his beret!

TA-DAH!

Suddenly he had an idea!

For the second time that day,
Claude shook his hat out on to
the floor. He grabbed the hose
and started hoofing through the
rainwater across the room.

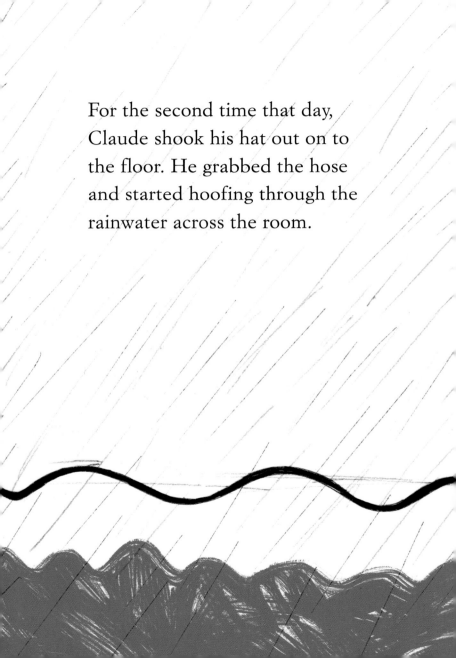

'No, don't add more water to
the problem, Claude!' cried Sir
Bobblysock from on high.

But Claude wasn't going to do that.

In no time at all Claude had
reached Great Granny, and
boy was she glad to see him!
Everyone went wild. They
hooted and clapped and cheered.

He waggled the hose about a few times, then threw it up into the air... where it tangled itself up around the chandelier. Then he started to climb!

Sir Bobblysock could hardly bear to look, but he asked Great Granny to clean his specs on her frock so he could get a better view of the action.

Claude smiled his nice smile. He was just about to tie some of the hose around Great Granny's waist to very gently lower her and Sir Bobblysock down to the ground when Princess Tiara Sparkles shouted,

'WAIT!'

Everyone goggled.

'Is there any way you can fix the hole in the roof?' Princess Sparkles said. 'Otherwise the entire palace will be flooded!'

Just as she said
it, the hole got
bigger... making
the chandelier
wobble like a jelly.

Claude HAD to fix
the roof! But what
could he do? AH
HA! His toolbox
was in his beret!

In his Outdoor Voice,
Claude asked Princess
Debonaire to open it...

But it was 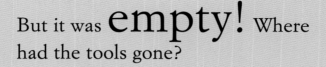empty! Where had the tools gone?

Sir Bobblysock gasped. 'I spent yesterday morning polishing them,' he cried. 'I wanted to use them to make myself a nice necklace to wear when we promenade around the duck pond in the park!'

So the tools were now lovely and clean, but at home.

Claude looked at what was left. A catapult, a surfboard, a spatula and some jam tarts. You couldn't possibly fix a hole in the roof with those...

OR COULD YOU?

Claude excitedly called down
some instructions to the Royal
Children, who got straight to work.

The guests watched in amazement
as Prince Beaudesert tied the
surfboard to the hose rope and
Claude hauled it up to the
chandelier.

Then Princess Debonaire set up the catapult and Prince Bonaventure gave Prince Babyface the jam tarts.

Silence fell in the Great Hall.

'Ready!' cried Claude.

'Steady...' cried Claude.

'GO!' cried Great Granny.

'Oh!' said Claude. 'Yes! GO!'

PING! WHOOSH! went Prince Babyface. At the very last moment Claude caught him, and the baby threw the jam tarts as hard as he could at the roof.

SQUELCH!

SQUELCH!

SQUELCH!

OOOSH!

The jam stuck like glue. Together,
Claude and Prince Babyface
stuck the surfboard over the hole.

77

Claude took a deep breath just to check, then – HURRAH! – the roof was fixed!

Everyone clapped and whooped again. Claude grabbed the hose rope to start getting everyone down from the chandelier, but...

UH OH! It was now very slippery with water, and it slipped right out of his hands. Oops!

'We'll have to jump!' said Claude.

Sir Bobblysock's lacy cap trembled. 'But we shall bump our bottoms when we land!' he said.

Claude had
another idea!

79

WEEEEEEEEEEEEEEEEE!

They flew through
the air... landing safely
and with a splat in Mr
Lovelybuns's giant cake!

The icing went everywhere,
but nowhere more so than all
over Great Granny. The room
fell silent again.

81

'Well,' said Great Granny sternly, 'I have never been to a party like this!'

Claude combed his ears sheepishly. 'Princess Sparkles was right,' he said. 'We aren't REALLY royal nannies. We were out looking for a nice elevenses treat when we heard Princess Sparkles say, "OH DEAR!" three times.

We just wanted to
help everyone. I'm
really very sorry.'

Great Granny glared
at Claude and Sir
Bobblysock.

83

Then all of a sudden she started to giggle! 'Sorry?' she hooted. 'Oh, you mustn't be sorry! One's never been to a party like this one – this is the best party ever! You and the Royal Children have given us the most wonderful, exciting entertainment AND you saved me and the palace!'

Everyone clapped and cheered.

84

'It has been *very* jolly!' said
Princess Tiara Sparkles.
'I just wonder how we can
ever thank you. Won't you
come and live at the
palace with us all?'

'You could be our new nanny!'
said Prince Bonaventure.
'You're ever such a lot of fun!'

Claude thought about it. He did like it at the palace – and he had enjoyed playing with the Royal Children. Then he looked at Sir Bobblysock.

Poor Sir Bobblysock! All the excitement had left him as limp as a Sunday afternoon and the damp **had** made his curls go all floppy.

Claude explained he had to take his friend home and get him well wrapped up in his shawls again. Everyone was disappointed, but they understood.

Claude and Sir Bobblysock did promise that they would definitely come back again to play, although preferably on a day when it wasn't raining.

'Well,' said Great Granny, 'the very least we can do is give you each a great big slice of cake to go home with. You never did get your elevenses!'

Claude and Sir Bobblysock liked that idea a lot. They were very hungry after all the excitement.

So, carrying a big glitzy box full of cake tied up with royal ribbons, Claude and Sir Bobblysock said goodbye to their new friends and splashed off.

Later that evening, Mr and Mrs
Shinyshoes were very surprised to
find great splodgy puddles all over
their kitchen when they came home
– and cake crumbs everywhere!

'Where on earth has this all come from?' asked Mrs Shinyshoes. 'You don't think Claude knows anything about it, do you?'

Mr Shinyshoes laughed. 'Of course he doesn't!' he said. 'Look! Claude's been fast asleep all day!'

But Claude DID know
something about it...

And we do too, don't we?

HRH CLAUDE AND HRH SIR BOBBLYSOCK'S GUIDE TO THROWING A ROYAL TEA PARTY

• Nice things to eat are sandwiches and cakes and scones and jam and cream.

• Make sure all the crusts are cut off the sandwiches so they are Most Dainty.

• Use a napkin to dab at the corners of your mouth after you have scoffed a bun or two.

• When you have a sip of your drink remember to stick your little finger out.

• Good things to say (in your Outdoor Voice) whilst eating are: "THESE SCONES ARE SPIFFING!" And also "GOODNESS ME THIS CAKE IS JOLLY MOIST!"